C

con

D1146742

We hope you enjoy your chosen book at home.

Dazzling
Danny

ROARING GOOD READS

Collins

Roaring Good Reads will fire the imagination of all young readers – from short stories for children just starting to read on their own, to first chapter books and short novels for confident readers.

www.roaringgoodreads.co.uk

Also by Jean Ure:

Daisy May

Monster in the Mirror

Big Tom

Other Roaring Good Reads from Collins

Witch-in-Training: Flying Lessons by *Maeve Friel*

Mister Skip by *Michael Morpurgo*

The Witch's Tears by *Jenny Nimmo*

Spider McDrew by *Alan Durant*

Dazzling Danny

JEAN URE

illustrated by
Karen Donnelly

An imprint of HarperCollins*Publishers*

First published in Great Britain by CollinsChildren'sBooks in 2003
Collins is an imprint of HarperCollins*Publishers* Ltd,
77-85 Fulham Palace Road, Hammersmith, London W6 8JB

The HarperCollins website address is www.**fire**and**water**.com

3 5 7 9 8 6 4 2

Text © Jean Ure 2003
Illustrations © Karen Donnelly 2003

The author and illustrator assert the moral right to be
identified as the author and illustrator of this work.

ISBN 0 00 713370 7

Printed and bound in England by
Clays Ltd, St Ives plc

Chapter One

Hi! I'm Danny Allbright. Dazzling Danny! That's what they call me. Dazzling Danny, or Danny the Dazzle. Sometimes just Dazzler. It really used to embarrass me when they first started doing it. That was back last term. The spring term. We're nearly at the end of summer, now, so I guess I've kind of got used to it. It doesn't bother me any more. Even my dad sometimes goes, "Hey! Dazzler!" And on my birthday my gran sent me a card that said, "To Danny the Dazzle." Trust Gran! She always gets things wrong. She's a really funny lady.

Anyway, about this dazzle thing. It all began one morning when Miss Pringle, who's our class teacher, said she wanted to talk to us.

"About the show."

Year 6 always do a show at the end of the spring term. Last year it had been *Charlie and the Chocolate Factory*. That was brilliant! I went to see it with Mum and Dad. I wished it could be *Charlie and the Chocolate Factory* again this year, so I could play Charlie, but Miss Pringle said that this year we were going to do something new. Something that had been written specially for us by Mr Hubbard. Mr Hubbard takes Year 5. He's OK, I quite like him, but I didn't think he could write anything as good as *Charlie and the Chocolate Factory*.

I looked across at Darryl, and pulled a face. Darryl pulled one back. I was sitting at a table with three others. Darryl Tyson, who is my best friend; Clint Parker, who is my worst enemy; and Joseph Brodrick, who is quite boring (but otherwise not bad).

Miss Pringle began telling us about the show. Her eyes were all shiny. She was really excited, you could tell. The show was going to be called *Go For It*! which I have to say is quite a good title. At any rate, it made me and Darryl sit up properly and start listening.

"It's a musical," said Miss Pringle.

Yeah! Me and Darryl kicked each other under the table. Musical was OK.

"It's all about *getting somewhere*."

Clint immediately yelled, "You wanna get somewhere? Try taking the bus!"

Some of the girls groaned. Coral Cookson turned round and hissed, "Shut your mouth, Clint Parker!" Miss Pringle just acted like he'd never said anything. He's a very annoying sort of person.

"The message is," said Miss Pringle, "that we can all get somewhere if we just... *go for it*! What is important is to have a goal... Something to aim for. You want to be a footballer? *Go for it*! Want to be a popstar? *Go for it*! Want to be a—"

"Teacher!" said Clint, and made a rude trumpeting noise down his nose. Everybody laughed; even me. I didn't want to, but I couldn't help it. Clint can be quite funny sometimes.

Miss Pringle didn't seem to mind. She said, "Thank you, Clint! Good suggestion. I'll bear it in mind."

Lucy Flowers wanted to know what everyone else was going to do. "The ones that aren't dreaming of being things."

Miss Pringle said that everyone else would be, like, a backing group. "There to give encouragement and to show that it can be done... if you just *go for it*. So!" She looked down at a sheet of paper she was holding. "We'd like you all to be in it, though you'll have to get your parents' permission, of course. Don't worry if you can't sing or dance, there are lots of speaking parts as well. This is what we thought... *singers*."

From her sheet of paper she read out eight names. I wasn't one of them, but that was all right. I can't sing! My mum always stuffs her fingers in her ears when I try to sing. Next, Miss Pringle read out the names of six dancers. I certainly wasn't one of them! Dancing wasn't my scene. No way! The six dancers were all girls. Clint Parker immediately objected. He shouted out, in a loud voice, "Why's it all girls?"

"It doesn't have to be," said Miss Pringle. "I'd be delighted to have some boys! Do you want to volunteer?"

That scared him! He kept quiet for the next few minutes.

"I only chose girls because I happen to know that these six all take dancing lessons," said Miss Pringle. "But if there are any boys..."

She gazed hopefully about the room. Darryl stuck his elbow in my ribs: I stuck mine in his. Darryl could volunteer if he liked! I wasn't going to.

"No one?" Miss Pringle sounded disappointed, but not particularly surprised. "All right! Let's move on to the speakers."

I relaxed. I didn't mind being a speaker! Miss Pringle read out the names.

"Lucy Flowers, Joseph Brodrick, Sheralee Johnson..."

She came to the end – and I wasn't there! I was the only person in the whole class who hadn't got a part! I knew I couldn't sing or dance, but I could speak all right. Why hadn't she included me?

Darryl kicked me again under the table. He'd noticed that I'd been left out. Even Darryl was one of the speakers! He's useless at reading out loud;

far worse than I am. But even he was going to be in the show!

And then Miss Pringle said, "Danny!" and everyone turned and looked at me, including Clint, who crossed his eyes and stuck out his tongue. "There's something special that I want Danny to do. But we're going to have to talk about it, so I'd like you to come and see me afterwards. All right?"

Clint went, "All right?" in a silly sort of voice. He was one of the speakers, too. I was suddenly glad that I wasn't going to be a speaker. I was going to be something special!

I spent the rest of the class wondering what it could possibly be and why Miss Pringle wanted to talk about it. What could I do that no one else could? Nothing, as far as I knew. I was the only one in my family who wasn't

gifted. My mum and dad both run for the county. Dad runs long distance, Mum's a

 sprinter. They've both won medals. They've even been given special Achievement Awards by the Mayor. My sister Carrie, who is one big pain, is brilliant at practically everything. She's two years older than me. Her last school report said, "Carrie works hard and plays hard. A first-class student!"

I just bet nobody would ever say that about me. Only the other day Miss Pringle had told me to stop daydreaming and pay attention. But now she wanted me to do something special!

Miss Pringle was busy telling us how the

Year 5s were going to paint the scenery and the Year 4s were going to design the programmes. Last year we had been Year 5s and had painted scenery. Clint Parker had painted two of the girls bright green. This year we were the big shots. We were the stars! And Miss Pringle wanted me for something special...

The bell rang for break. All the rest of the class went rushing out into the playground, but Miss Pringle beckoned me over to her table.

"Now then, Danny," she said. "We must talk. There are two very important parts that I didn't mention... one boy, and one girl. These are the ones who have all the dreams.

We've already cast Coral as the girl—"

She paused, just for a second. I waited, breathlessly. Was she really going to say what I thought she was going to say?

"Both Mr Hubbard and I," said Miss Pringle, "think that you would be perfect as the boy."

Wow! Maybe I *was* good at something, after all.

"The only thing is," said Miss Pringle, "it does mean that you would have to dance..."

Chapter Two

Dance???

Miss Pringle tilted her head to one side. "How would you feel about it?"

How I felt about it was, *you've got to be kidding*! Only you can't say that to a teacher.

"What do you think?" said Miss Pringle.

"If I don't do it," I said, "does that mean I can't be in the show?"

"Oh, Danny, of course it doesn't! Of course you'll be in the show."

I said, "What would I be?"

"How about one of the speakers?"

I frowned. I didn't want to be one of the speakers! Not if Clint was going to be. I wanted to be something special.

"Look, don't get all worried about it," said Miss Pringle. "We can find someone else if we have to."

I didn't want that, either! That would mean that someone else was special. Instead of me. It might even be Clint!

"It's just that we really do feel you'd be good at it. You're a nice little mover! You've got a lot of style. Did you know that?"

I didn't know what to say. My mum always tells me that I'm like a tornado. She says that one of these days the roof will cave in, the way I crash around. Now Miss Pringle was saying I had style!

"I was watching you, the other day," said Miss Pringle, "when you were playing football."

I said, "Yeah, well... football." That was different.

"If you watch the really top players," said Miss Pringle, "you'll see they move very much the same way as dancers do."

I didn't want to be rude or anything, so I just kept quiet.

"I'll tell you what," said Miss Pringle.

"Tomorrow after school we'll go through some of the steps together, just you and me, not anyone else, and you can decide whether you want to do it or not. How about that? Would that be a good idea, do you think?"

I nodded.

"All right, then. Don't forget to ask your mum if it's OK. Tell her we'll just be about half an hour."

As soon as I hit the playground, Darryl came charging over.

"So what was it? What's she want you to do?"

I mumbled, "Wants me to do something special."

"Like what?"

"Just something."

I wasn't even going to tell Darryl, in spite of him being my best friend. Not until I'd made up my mind.

I said to Mum that I had to stay late at school the next day. I said it was something to do with the library. Mum's quite keen on books so she said that was fine.

"I'll come by half an hour later."

I wasn't even going to tell Mum the real reason. She'd only go and tell Dad, and I *definitely* didn't want Dad to know.

Next day, at the end of school, I went to the hall. Miss Pringle was there waiting for me. She was wearing a T-shirt and joggers. I like it when she dresses like that! She looks cool; not like a teacher. She said, "OK, Danny! Football number. I'll show you what we had in mind." Then she put on some music and started to dance.

She's really good! Like something off the telly. I never knew Miss Pringle could dance like that. It's a spiky kind of dancing. Zip, zap! Leap, spin. Now she's crouched low, snapping her fingers. Now she's up in the air, *wham!*

As I stand watching her, my feet start to tap. They do it all by themselves. Miss Pringle jerks forward – and so do I. Miss

Pringle does a little hop – so do I. By the time she stops, I'm jigging about like some kind of glove puppet.

"Well!" She comes over to me. A bit out of breath, but not much. "What do you think? Do you feel like giving it a go?"

I said, "Um..."

It was like my mind was telling me *no* while my body was going *yes*. I didn't want to be a dancer! But my feet were doing their own thing, twitching and tapping to the beat of the music. I couldn't seem to stop them. Then my fingers started snapping and my legs started springing and I was following Miss Pringle, doing what she was doing. Zip, zap! Leap, spin!

"Danny, that is so good!"

I'd been in Miss Pringle's class for a whole

term and she'd never, ever praised me before.
Not like that. The most she'd ever said was,
"Well done, Danny! Top marks for trying."

Now it was like I didn't have to try. My
body was doing it all for me.

"See?" Miss Pringle beamed. A great big beam that spread across her face. "I knew you could do it! And you enjoyed it, didn't you? Don't tell me you didn't!"

I grinned. I couldn't help it.

"So what shall we do?" said Miss Pringle. "Shall we put you down as the Boy?"

I wanted to yell, "*Yes!*" But there was still this little bit of me that wasn't quite sure.

"What do you reckon?" said Miss Pringle.

I said, "Well... yeah. OK. I guess."

Miss Pringle was really pleased. She told me I'd made the right choice.

"It's what it's all about... *going for it*. Doing the things

28

you're good at. Because who knows where it might lead?"

She gave me a slip of paper that either Mum or Dad had to sign. I knew at once that that slip of paper was going to be a problem. I didn't want Mum or Dad to know what I was doing! Mum and Dad were athletes. They'd always expected me and Carrie to be athletes, too. How could I tell them I was *dancing*? I knew that I couldn't. But I had to get that bit of paper signed! Miss Pringle wouldn't let me be in the show if I didn't get it signed. And I really wanted to be in the show. I wanted to be something special!

All the way home in the car I was very quiet. Mum wondered if I wasn't feeling well. I am not usually quiet. At school I am always getting told off for talking.

"I hope you're not sickening for something," said Mum.

I wasn't sickening: I was thinking. I was thinking how to get my bit of paper signed. I'd had an idea...

The minute I'd finished tea, I galloped upstairs to my sister's room. I knew she was in there as she was playing music, very loud. She always plays music when she does her homework.

"Carrie?" I knocked on the door. You have to knock on the door or she gets really mad. She got mad anyway. Her voice came bawling out at me.

"*What d'you want?*"

"Want to ask you something."

"What?"

"Can I come in?"

"No!"

"*Please?*"

She let me in the end, though she grumbled about it.

"I'm busy," she said. "What is it?"

I showed her my slip of paper. "Could you sign Mum's name on here for me?"

Carrie said, "Why?"

"'Cos it's for the end of term show and I want it to be a secret, and if you sign it," I said, "I'll give you something."

"What?"

I said, "I'll give you... 20p!"

"*20p*?" said Carrie. "You have to be joking!"

"50p?"

"Joking!"

In desperation, I said, "I'll do your turn at cleaning the car!"

"And I get to keep the money?" said Carrie.

I had to say yes, or she wouldn't have signed. She's a very grasping sort of person.

But she's ace at doing Mum's signature! I think she'll probably be a forger when she grows up.

Signed: Mrs. Allbright

Next day, I gave the slip of paper to Miss Pringle.

"Wonderful!" said Miss Pringle.

I still wasn't sure.

Chapter Three

I remember it was on a Friday we had our first rehearsal. The reason I remember is that while Miss Pringle was telling us where to go, Clint Parker flipped a rubber across the room and hit Lucy Flowers on the head. Lucy shrieked, and Clint was sent out. As he went he shouted, "See if I care! It's Saturday tomorrow. No more school, *yeeee-eah*!"

Miss Pringle just carried on like nothing had happened. She told us that the dancers were to go to the Big Hall, the singers to the Small Hall, and the speakers should stay in the classroom. I got up to leave, and Darryl said, "Where you off to?"

"Going to rehearsal," I said.

"Speakers are in here," said Darryl.

"Yeah," I said, "I know."

"So where're you going?"

There are times when Darryl can be *so nosy*. But we usually tell each other everything, so I suppose I couldn't really blame him.

"You're not going with the *girls*?" he said.

He knew I couldn't be going with the

singers. I said that I would tell him later and ran off before he could ask any more questions.

Miss Pringle took the dance rehearsal. We started off doing the steps she'd shown me just the other day. I could remember them quite clearly, and even the order they came in. The girls were well impressed! They didn't know I'd already learnt them, and Miss Pringle didn't let on. Some of the girls were really slow. Leanne Walters, for instance, and Saru Sathay. They had to go over and over the same steps, and still couldn't get them right. The only one who picked them up as quickly as I had was Coral. She was good! Coral was playing the other lead part. She was the Girl, I was the Boy. Miss Pringle said that she was going to give us some special numbers to do on our own.

"Just the two of you... I'll work out something exciting!"

I'd been a bit anxious in case any of the girls might laugh, me being the only boy, but none of them did. They didn't seem to think there was anything peculiar about it. It's funny, with girls. There are times they can be just *so-o-o* superior, like when they gang up on you and giggle. It's very off-putting, when they do that. But then at other times they can be quite nice. I am not really sure that I understand them properly. Mum says that one day I will. (Dad says you never do!)

Darryl was waiting for me as we came out of the hall. He gave me this odd look.

"Never knew you could dance," he said.

I told him that Miss Pringle had made me. "I didn't want to! She said I'd got to."

I wasn't sure whether he believed me or not. I mean, teachers *can* make you do things. They make you do things all the time. But they don't usually make people take part in end of term shows if people don't want to.

"She'd have been upset," I muttered. "I was the only one she could find."

"Way out!" said Darryl.

But Darryl is my friend. He is OK! What I was dreading was when Clint found out. I knew that he would, because there wasn't any way of keeping it secret. Not that I really cared about Clint. Not really. The people I most wanted to keep it from were Mum and Dad.

Every weekend, me, Mum and Dad would all go running round the park. I don't

specially like running; I found it a bit boring,
to be honest. I had these landmarks. Run,
run, run... oak tree. Run, run... clump of
nettles. Run, run... litter bin. Run, run...

broken fence. Sometimes I counted, one, two, three, four... seeing if it came to the same number every time. Sometimes I made up footie teams. Now I started going over dance steps, feeling them in my feet as I ran. The only trouble was, it made me want to stop running and start dancing! I had to be careful, because Mum always made sure to hang back and keep an eye on me. She hoped that one day I might join the Athletics Club and get on to a team.

The only reason I went on running was to keep Mum and Dad happy. Carrie had given it up. She'd suddenly said one morning that she didn't want to do it any more. "It's just a waste of time!" Carrie didn't seem to mind about hurting Mum and Dad's feelings. She'd announced the other day that she was going to be a doctor when she grew up. Mum had cried, "Oh, that's a great idea! Then you could specialise in sports injuries."

Carrie had made this impatient scoffing noise and said, "I don't want to have anything to *do* with sports!"

Mum's face had fallen. I had felt really sorry for her! I'd heard her telling Dad later, and Dad had said, "We must let her do her own thing." Sadly, Mum had agreed. And then she had cheered up and said, "There's always Danny! He's still enjoying it."

This was why I didn't want them to know about the dancing. I thought they might think it was a bit cissy.

Clint thought it was cissy, but then he would. He thinks reading books is cissy. He thinks everything is cissy that doesn't involve fighting. He came prancing up to me on Monday morning with his hands all limp, going, "*Girly! Girly!*" I tried to do what Miss Pringle does and pretend he wasn't there, but he stuck his face in mine and went, "Girly

wirly! Girly wirly!" Coral
was with me. She's quite
tough, is Coral. I think
she must have learnt
kick boxing because
next thing I know her
leg's flying through the
air and Clint's staggering
backwards, howling as
he goes.

"You just leave
people alone!" yelled
Coral. "You're an
idiot!"

After that, he only
had a go at me when
Coral wasn't around. I
didn't really care about

Clint; like Coral said, he was an idiot. But I did worry about Mum and Dad! I didn't like keeping things from them. I specially didn't like having to tell lies. It wasn't something I'd ever done before. I mean, OK, I'd told them *little* lies. Like it wasn't me that left the bathroom tap running, and I had no idea how muddy footprints had got on the sitting-room carpet. That sort of thing. But not huge walloping lies like, "I'm staying late at school because of library duty," or computer club, or book circle.

Carrie got to know about it. She would! She came up to me and said, "Why are you pretending to be doing things when you aren't really?"

I said, "What do you mean, I'm not really?"

"You're dancing in the show!" said Carrie.

I scowled at her. "How d'you know?"

"I know everything," said Carrie.

I knew how she knew. Leanne's sister was in her class. That was how she knew.

"Why don't you just tell them?" said Carrie.

I said, "'Cos I don't want to, and you're not to, either!"

Carrie looked at me, with her head to one side. "What'll you give me to keep quiet?"

I said, "Nothing!" I'd already cleaned the car for her. What more did she want?

"Do my share of the housework for... the next five days! Then I won't tell on you."

It is terrible to have a sister like that.

One day after rehearsal, while me and Coral were waiting for our mums to collect us, I said, "I'm not sure I ought to be doing this."

"Doing what?" said Coral.

I said, "Dancing." One boy, and six girls...

"Why not?" said Coral. "I'm doing it!"

I said, "It's different for you."

"Why? Just 'cos I'm a *girl*?"

I thought about it. Coral is my second-best friend after Darryl. She is all right, even though she is a girl. I mean, I do quite like girls; except, as I say, when they get together and giggle at you. But they don't always understand what it is like to be a boy.

I said this to Coral. I said, "I'm not being *anti-girl.*"

"Oh, no?" said Coral.

"No! But... it's my mum and dad."

"What's the matter with your mum and dad?"

I said, "They're not like yours."

"Oh," jeered Coral, "you mean my mum and dad are ordinary people and yours are famous!"

"They're athletes," I said. "They might think it's... well! Cissy."

"Do you think it is?" said Coral.

I hung my head. "I dunno."

I thought that it might be all right if I wasn't the only boy. But *six girls*...

"I can't imagine Clint," I muttered.

"Clint's an idiot," said Coral. "He's Stone Age!"

I said, "Yeah, I know, but— "

"All that matters," said Coral, "is if you enjoy it. Do you enjoy it?"

I nodded. I did enjoy it! Sometimes I got ashamed and thought I shouldn't, but I did!

Specially the number that I was doing with Coral.

"Well, there you are, then," said Coral. "What's the problem?"

Like I said, girls don't always understand how it feels to be a boy.

Chapter Four

It is not easy, keeping secrets from your mum
and dad. For one thing, they are always asking
questions. *So how is the computer club? What are
you reading in your book circle? Are you still on
library duty?* You have to tell them all these lies
and it makes you feel really bad. Plus it is not

good for your nerves, as you expect every minute that you will be found out.

One day, when I was waiting with Coral after rehearsal, our mums both turned up at the same moment. My mum pulled up in her car just as Coral's mum was pulling up in hers. They both got out. They started *talking*. I was really scared because Coral was still wearing her dance gear. She'd got this bright pink leotard thing, and shiny tights. She didn't look in the least like a person that had just taken part in a book circle (which was what I'd told Mum we were doing). She looked like a person that had just been at a dance rehearsal. I had to act – quickly!

I yelled, "*Mum*," and went shooting off across the playground.

"What's the big rush?" said Mum.

"Gotta get back!" I panted. "Something I gotta watch!"

I went hurtling into the car, dragging Mum after me. Mum was quite cross. She told me that I had better mend my manners.

"That was an extremely rude way to behave!"

I didn't like Mum being cross with me, but at least she hadn't discovered my secret. I was safe for the moment – but not for very long. It was Darryl, next time, who nearly gave me away. Darryl's mum was going into hospital, just for one night, and Darryl was coming to sleep over at our place. He'd done it before. No problem! I liked having Darryl sleep over; we had a lot of fun together. But this time I was, like, walking on eggshells. I warned him not to mention the show. I *told* him.

"I don't want Mum and Dad to know about it! OK?"

Darryl was cool. He said, "Sure. OK!"

I didn't have to explain to him. He could understand why I didn't want Mum and Dad to know. But then he nearly went and blew it! We're sitting down having tea when all of a sudden, for absolutely no reason, he starts chanting some of his lines from the show.

"You can – DO it,

Anyone can – DO it.

Dream it, scheme it,

Man, I MEAN it!"

All the time he's chanting, he's beating on the table with his knife and fork.

"You can – DO it,

Anyone can – DO it."

Just, like, totally mindless. Mum laughed and said, "What's that?"

I immediately kicked out under the table. Darryl gave a yelp, but it brought him to his senses. He grinned this soppy grin and said, "Just something."

Carrie sang out, "*Go for it*!" and slid her eyes towards me. I kicked her, too. Carrie snarled, "Do you mind?"

Mum said, "Oh, please, you two! Don't start."

A bad moment! Sometimes I really wondered if it was worth it. All this hassle just to be something special? I kept thinking that I would tell Miss Pringle I didn't want to do it any more. Every time I went to a rehearsal I made up my mind that I was definitely going to tell her. Once I even got as far as saying, "Miss! I—" And then I stopped and got tongue-tied. Miss Pringle said, "What is it, Danny?" I said, "Um—"

"Tell me afterwards," said Miss Pringle.

But afterwards was too late. By the time we finished rehearsing, the rhythm had got into my feet and they didn't want to stop. It was like they had a life of their own. I had to tell Miss Pringle *before* we started rehearsing. Before my feet got all twitchy.

I made this vow that I would do it next

weekend, for sure. But then next weekend came and Miss Pringle started talking about costumes and everyone got excited. The girls were going to wear shiny tights and leotards in all different colours. I said, "Like a rainbow," and Miss Pringle said, "Yes! Exactly! Now, what about you and Coral? We thought perhaps if you had a yellow top, with red tights, and Coral had a red top, with yellow tights... what do you think?

I nearly fell over when she said tights. I said, "*Tights*?"

Coral giggled. She said, "*Tights*?" She was mimicking me. She's very good at mimicking. She said, "Shock, horror! *Tights*!" and all the others giggled, too.

Miss Pringle said, "Oh, now, come on! Don't let's be silly about it. I expect better of you than this sort of childish nonsense."

That was when I should have told her. I should have said, "I'm not going to wear tights! I don't want to do this any more!" But I couldn't. She was all happy and burbling, going on about how red and yellow would look good against all the other colours. It would have hurt her if I'd said I didn't want to wear her stupid costume or do her stupid show. But I had to find a way to get out of it! I couldn't have my dad seeing me in tights...

I said this to Coral, while we were waiting for our mums. Coral just said, "Danny Allbright, you're an idiot!" and went racing off across the playground, leaving me standing there. I thought she might have been a bit more sympathetic. She was supposed to be my *friend*.

I got very desperate. There were only three weeks to go before the dress rehearsal. I had to do something! But what?

In the middle of the night, this brilliant idea came to me. I would fall down some steps and break a bone! Nobody could be expected to dance with a broken bone. I would be saved!

The best steps I could think of were the ones in the back garden, leading down from the patio. There were six of them, and they were made of concrete. Really hard! If I hurled myself madly down them, surely *something* would break? Even just an arm would be enough. Even just a wrist. Just a *finger*.

I decided that I would do it on Saturday morning, when Mum and Dad were there, because then they could take me to the hospital. I quite fancied the idea of going in to school on Monday with my arm in plaster; or better still, walking on crutches. Everyone would go "Ooh!" and "Aah" and "How did you do it?" And Miss Pringle would be sorry that I couldn't do her dancing for her, but at least she wouldn't be hurt. I'd be the one that was hurt! Only I wouldn't mind.

Saturday morning I went into the garden and stood at the top of the steps. I'd thought it would be quite simple to hurl myself down them, but I think perhaps I am not very brave. At the last moment I got cold feet. Suppose I broke my *neck*? I might never be able to walk again!

I was still dithering when Carrie and her friend Jade Sullivan came screaming through the patio door. They're always screaming, that pair. And they *never* bother to look where they're going. I didn't have to hurl myself because those two great clumsy girls went and barged into me and sent me sprawling. *Thump, bang, clonk*, down to the bottom of the steps.

"What are you doing?" bawled Carrie. Like it was my fault.

Carefully, I picked myself up. I patted at myself. All over. Arms, legs, ribs. Nothing! Not even as much as a bruise. I hadn't even broken a finger!

"Just look where you're standing in future!" shrieked Carrie.

Perhaps I should have got the spade out of the garden shed and told her to whack me with it. She'd probably have broken both legs for me straight off.

Chapter Five

One morning, driving in to school, Mum said to me, "Aren't you having a show this term?"

I said, "Sh–show?" Like it was some foreign word I'd never heard before.

Mum said, "Yes! Show! You know? Singing, dancing, acting... *end of term show*?"

"Oh! That," I said.

Then there was this long pause, while Mum waited for me to go on and I tried to think of something to say.

"It isn't any good this year," I mumbled.

"Really?" said Mum. "Why's that?"

"Dunno. Just isn't. Not worth coming to."

"Don't be silly," said Mum, "of course we'll come! If you're going to be in it."

"Yeah, well, this is it," I said. "I'm not."

"Oh?" Mum sounded surprised. "I thought they always included everyone?"

"Not always," I said. "It's just singing and dancing this year."

"Well, you certainly can't sing," agreed Mum.

"Can't dance, either," I said.

"So you're not in it?"

I said, "No. Hey, look, there's Darryl!" I opened the window and stuck my head out. "Oy! Darryl!"

Darryl saw me, and waved. Mum let me out the car. She said, "Off you go, then," and I tore across the pavement and through the gates. Phew! Another escape!

Mum didn't say anything more about the show, so I hoped she'd forgotten it. I thought that if she asked me again I'd say it was too late to get tickets, they'd all been sold. But then something else happened. Miss Pringle said that next Wednesday we were going to have the dress rehearsal, and that this would mean staying on at school for an extra two hours. She gave us all a note to give to our mums and dads, for them to sign. I didn't know what to do! I could get Carrie to sign Mum's name, no problem; but next Wednesday my gran was flying home from Jamaica and we were all going to the airport to meet her. I didn't want to miss seeing my gran!

I told Coral about it, thinking that she would understand. Coral had been really upset last year, when her gran had died. She'd loved her gran as much as I love mine.

"I've got to go and meet her!" I said.

"Why?" said Coral. "You'll see her when you get home."

I said, "I won't! We're taking her back to her place."

"Well, you'll see her in the holidays," said Coral.

"I want to see her *now*," I said. "She's been away for nearly two months!"

"You can't miss the dress rehearsal," said Coral.

"But what am I going to tell my mum and dad?"

Coral said, "That's your problem! Maybe you could try telling them the truth, for a change?"

Girls can be really hard at times. Really unfeeling.

"What about *me*?" said Coral.

What about her?

"What about our *pas de deux*?"

"Oh! *Pardy durr*," I said, mimicking her like she'd mimicked me.

Coral's cheeks grew very hot and pink. I knew that I'd been mean, but she'd been mean to me! Did she really think our stupid dance was more important than my gran?

"I might decide not to do it at all," I said.

Coral looked at me, horrified. "You can't back out *now*!"

"Yes, I can," I said. "I can do what I like. I don't have to be in the show if I don't want to."

"If you didn't want to do it," cried Coral, "you should have said so right back at the beginning." She made this little choking sound. "You'll just go and ruin it for everyone!"

Now she was starting to cry. I hate when they do that!

"You're just being mean and selfish and – and *cowardly*!" Tears went rolling down her cheeks. She wiped them away, angrily, with the back of her hand. "Danny Allbright," she said, "if you back out of the show I'll never speak to you again!"

Huh! What did I care? She was only a girl.

I said this to Darryl, next day, as we mooched round the playground together. Darryl was my best friend! Surely he would understand?

"So you mean... you're not coming to the dress rehearsal?" said Darryl.

"I've got to meet my gran," I said. "She's old! She mightn't live much longer."

Darryl has met my gran. "She's not as old as all that," he said. "She could live for years!"

"But what would I tell my mum and dad?"

"Dunno," said Darryl.

He wasn't being at all helpful.

"Wish I'd never agreed to be in the stupid show," I said.

"Bit late for that now," said Darryl.

"I could still drop out! If I wanted to. I think I probably will," I said.

Darryl gave me this *look*. Like I was a bit of bird splodge, or something nasty that had crawled out of a bin.

"Not surprised Coral said she wouldn't speak to you again."

"Think I care?" I said.

"Not sure I'd want to speak to you again, either," said Darryl; and he turned, and went running off across the playground to join some of the others in a football game.

I thought that Darryl was being very

unfair. It is no way for a person's best friend to treat them.

When I got in after school my sister was there. She was in a really annoying mood. She kept snapping her fingers and waggling her hips and singing "*GO for it! Just – GO for it!*" and giving me these sly looks. I shoved at her and she fell against the corner of the sink and screamed, "Ow! That hurt!" Mum told me crossly to stop behaving like a yob.

"I don't know what's come over you these days!"

She must have told Dad about it, because later that evening Dad said he wanted to speak to me, and he gave me this long lecture all about *manners*.

"I want you to be a tough guy, but I also want you to be a gentleman. Gentlemen do not go round pushing and shoving at their sisters. You got that?"

I nodded.

Dad said, "Right! I don't want to have to speak to you again."

Suddenly it just seemed like everyone had it in for me. At school next day, Coral wasn't talking. I pretended I didn't care, but I did, really. Coral's been my second-best friend ever since Reception, when she tried to stuff a marble in my ear.

Miss Pringle asked us all to hand in our slips of paper. I was the only one who hadn't got a signature...

"Oh, Danny, really!" said Miss Pringle. "How could you forget?"

Coral turned and looked at me. I said, "Sorry, Miss."

"Well, can you make sure and get it done tonight?" said Miss Pringle.

There was this long silence. Coral was still looking at me. I could feel that Darryl was, too.

"Yes?" said Miss Pringle.

I took a deep breath. I said, "Yes, Miss."

Darryl patted my shoulder. "It'll be all right," he said.

What did he mean, it would be all right? It was all right for him. He wasn't dancing with six girls. Wearing *tights*.

I had to ask Carrie to do more of her forging. She said, "Well, I will... but you owe me! Specially after last night." She said she wouldn't be at all surprised if I'd broken some of her ribs. She said a person could die of broken ribs, and if she died it would be all my fault. "So you can jolly well do my next *six turns* at cleaning the car!"

That was bad enough, but then I had to find some excuse for staying on at school and not going to meet Gran. It meant telling more lies, and one thing Gran has always taught us is that telling lies is "a slippery slope". In the end I decided just to tell half a lie. I mean, at least it was better than telling a whole one. I said that Miss Pringle was having the dress rehearsal and that she wanted me to help out backstage.

Mum said, "Oh, that's nice! I'm glad you're involved. Can you go back with Darryl afterwards and we'll pick you up from his place?"

What really made me mad was that I needn't have bothered asking Carrie to forge Mum's signature after all. Mum would have signed it herself. Now I was going to have to clean the car *six times* without being paid for it!

Chapter Six

Countdown. Four days, three days, two days, one day... lift off!

The morning of the show Mum said to me, "So you're going to be helping out backstage, then?"

I'd told her that once! I bent my head over

my cereal bowl and muttered, "Yeah."

"You mean, there's no point us coming along?" said Dad.

I'd told Mum that, as well!

"You couldn't come, anyway," I said. "Tickets'll be all gone."

"That's a pity," said Dad.

Why was it a pity? I looked at Dad, and frowned. He and Mum were behaving in a very odd way.

"I'm not *in* it," I said.

"How about Darryl?" said Mum. "Is he in it?"

"Yeah," I said. "Darryl's in it."

Surely they wouldn't want to go and see *Darryl*?

"I thought you said it was all singing and dancing?" said Mum.

"Mm." I made a mumbling sound, through a mouthful of toasty pops.

"So can Darryl sing and dance?"

I shook my head. "He's useless."

"So why is he in it and not you?"

Why do mums always have to ask so many questions? I said, "I dunno," and stuffed another spoonful of toasty pops into my mouth. Carrie giggled. I zapped her with laser beams across the table, but my sister is totally INSENSITIVE. In this very tuneless voice that she has, she started singing.

"*GO for it! Just – GO for it!*"

"What is this silly song you keep singing?" said Mum. "Is it the latest hit?"

This time, Carrie giggled so much she nearly fell off her chair. Darryl doesn't know how lucky he is, not having a sister.

The show didn't start until seven o'clock that evening, but Miss Pringle wanted us all to be there by half-past five. Darryl and his mum and dad were stopping by to pick me up. They were going to bring me back again, afterwards. As soon as I saw their car pull up, I went racing to the door. I didn't want Mum getting out there, talking to them.

"See you later," said Mum. "Hope it goes well!"

Dad then came to the door and called after me: "Break a leg!" I thought this was a strange sort of thing to say, until Darryl's dad explained that *break a leg* was a theatrical way of wishing someone good luck.

But why should Dad think that I needed good luck? I was only helping out backstage!

When we reached school, I almost wished that I was just helping out. I felt like a big wobbly jelly, trembling on a plate. And I couldn't remember a single one of my steps! I'd been practising them all day in my bedroom; and now, suddenly, they'd gone.

"You nervous?" I said to Darryl, as we made our way to the boys' changing room.

"What's to be nervous about?" said Darryl.

"Might forget your lines," I said.

"Only got two," said Darryl.

He meant that he only had two that he spoke by himself. It wouldn't matter if he forgot the rest, because they were spoken by everybody. Even I could remember two lines!

But I had whole long sequences of steps. Coral would never forgive me if I went and messed things up!

Clint was in the changing room. He'd already had a good laugh at me at the dress rehearsal, but he couldn't resist starting up again. He said, "Hallo, girly!" in this silly squeaky voice. "Sure you're in the right room? This one's for boys!"

Darryl snarled, "Shut your cakehole, dummy, or I'll shove your teeth down your throat!"

A bad moment! I couldn't let Darryl fight my battles for me, but I really didn't want a scrap. Not right then. Maybe later, but not before I'd done Miss Pringle's dancing for her. I didn't reckon she'd be very pleased if I went on stage with a black eye. Not that I'd have been the only one. Clint would have had one, too; you could count on that. Fortunately it didn't happen, because Clint backed down. Just as well! I would have thrashed him.

Lots of people had been sent Good Luck cards, which they stuck on the wall. To my surprise, my mum and dad had sent me one. They'd sent it to the school, and Mr Hubbard gave it to me when he came round to check we were all getting changed. I thought that was quite nice of them, though it did make me feel bad about all the lies I'd told. In spite of that, I was still glad they weren't there! If

Mum and Dad had been in the audience, I would have been too embarrassed to dance.

I was embarrassed enough as it was. The thought of going out there, in front of all those people, wearing tights and *dancing* – with six girls! Plus I still wasn't sure I could remember any of the steps. My head felt like a big ball of cotton wool. My legs felt like strips of spaghetti. And I *couldn't remember what I had to do*.

It was Coral who rescued me. As I stood there shaking in the wings, waiting to go on, she whispered, "Just do what your feet tell you!"

She said afterwards that it was what her dance teacher had once said to her when she was in a panic. And it worked! I stopped trying to *think* and just let my feet do their own thing. My feet were brilliant! They did it all by themselves.

"Told you so," hissed Coral.

She was rather cocky about it, but I forgave her. Her and me got the biggest round of applause of anyone! At the end, we had to take a bow all by ourselves.

"Man," said Darryl, clapping me on the back, "that was great! I bet you're glad, now, that your mum and dad came."

I looked at him, in horror. I said, "*What*?"

"Your mum and dad," said Darryl. "They're out there... didn't you see them? Sitting in the front row, next to mine."

Mum and Dad – and Carrie – had been there all the time! It was my sister's fault.

"I'm sorry," she said. "They got it out of me."

Mum and Dad couldn't understand why I'd tried to keep it from them.

"What do you think we are?" said Mum.

"Monsters?" said Dad.

"It's nothing to be ashamed of."

"We're *proud* of you!"

I didn't believe them. I thought they were

just saying it, to make me feel better. I still didn't believe them even when my gran rang up and said, "What's all this I hear? My grandson the dancer? Stealing the show?"

"It wasn't me," I muttered. "It was Coral."

"That's not what I heard," said Gran. "I heard it was both of you. My! Wouldn't your granddad have been proud!"

Next day, the local newspaper came through the letterbox. And there, right on the front page where you couldn't help seeing it, was a big colour picture of me and Coral! Over the picture, in huge great capital letters, it said:

But it wasn't until Dad got a copy of the original photograph and had it framed and hung on the wall that I finally believed him. He and Mum were really proud of me! Just as proud as if I'd won the junior athletics trophy.

I got my sister to pay me back for all those times I'd cleaned the car for her. *And* I got her to do my share of the washing-up, the wiping-up and the vacuuming for the next two weeks.

I also bashed Clint the next time he called me girly. You have to stick up for yourself.

Now they all call me Dazzling Danny, but like I said, it doesn't really bother me. Danny the Dazzle... I can live with that!